My GOVERNMENT

Standing in the Speaker of the House's Shoes

Kaitlyn Duling

Cavendish Square
New York

Published in 2018 by Cavendish Square Publishing, LLC
243 5th Avenue, Suite 136, New York, NY 10016

First Edition

Library of Congress Cataloging-in-Publication Data

Names: Duling, Kaitlyn.
Title: Standing in the Speaker of the House's shoes / Kaitlyn Duling.
Description: New York : Cavendish Square, 2018. | Series: My government | Includes index.
Identifiers: ISBN 9781502630780 (pbk.) | ISBN 9781502630803 (library bound) | ISBN 9781502630797 (6 pack) | ISBN 9781502630810 (ebook)
Subjects: LCSH: United States. Congress. House--Speakers--Juvenile literature.
Classification: LCC JK1411.D85 2018 | DDC 328.73'0762--dc23

Editorial Director: David McNamara
Editor: Jodyanne Benson
Copy Editor: Nathan Heidelberger
Associate Art Director: Amy Greenan
Designer: Jessica Nevins
Production Coordinator: Karol Szymczuk
Photo Research: J8 Media

The photographs in this book are used by permission and through the courtesy of: Cover Martin Falbisoner/Wikimedia Commons/File:US Capitol west side.JPG; p. 4 Matt McClain/The Washington Post/Getty Images; p. 6 SAUL LOEB/AFP/Getty Images; p. 8 Zach Gibson/AP Images; p. 9 YURI GRIPAS/REUTERS/Newscom; p. 10, 21, 22 Chip Somodevilla/Getty Images; p. 12 Alex Wong/Getty Images; p. 14 Teresa Levite/Shutterstock.com; p. 15 Olivier Douliery/Getty Images; p. 16 Gregg Segal Photography; p. 17 Bill Clark/CQ Roll Call/Getty Images; p. 18 Bobby Caina Calvan/AP Images; p. 20 Irfan Khan/Los Angeles Times/Getty Images; p. 23 Richard Hutchings/Corbis/Getty Images; p. 24 Eric Thayer/Getty Images; p. 26 Sean Rayford/Getty Images; p. 27 Image Source/Getty Images.

Printed in the United States of America

TABLE OF CONTENTS

The Speaker's place is at the front of the House of Representatives.

INTRODUCTION

Laws do many things. They help keep us safe. They make sure we wear seat belts in the car. Laws keep us healthy. They keep our water clean. Laws protect the things we own. We need people to make these laws. Those who work in the United States government help our lives run smoothly by making and carrying out laws.

Without the people who work in Congress, we might not have schools! We might not have enough jobs. Our animals and parks could be at risk. Many people go to work on Capitol Hill each day. They do their best to make laws that will help everyone.

The former Speaker, Nancy Pelosi, shakes the hand of the new Speaker, Paul Ryan.

CHAPTER ONE

The Responsibilities of the Speaker of the House

Congress has two parts. The Senate is smaller. There are 100 senators. Each state has two senators. Then there is the House of Representatives. This part is big. It has 435 members! The Speaker is the leader of the House of Representatives. He or she helps out new members of Congress. He or she also gives them the **oath**. The oath of office is a promise. All members promise to do good work for the United States.

The Speaker also helps make **committees**. These are special groups. The groups work on laws and projects. The Speaker decides who will be in charge of each group.

The Speaker of the House gives the oath of office.

There are many of these in the House. There is one about money. There is another about schools. There is even one about farming! Each group is important. They think about laws and issues. Sometimes they are in charge of programs.

The Speaker also tells people when they can talk. He or she sits at the front of the House and sometimes holds

The Speaker helps make special groups, or committees.

a **gavel**. This is a wooden hammer. It is used to keep order. The Speaker of the House can smack it on the table when it gets too loud. Sometimes members of Congress are talking. Sometimes the noise comes from the gallery. This is where people sit to watch the House. If you visit Capitol Hill, you could sit in the gallery, too!

Sometimes the Speaker uses a gavel to help keep attention or quiet down the House.

The Speaker helps get things done. He or she calls the House to order and makes a plan for talking and voting. The Speaker of the House keeps the House on schedule. Sometimes he or she votes on laws. Usually, the Speaker does not vote.

The Speaker of the House is very busy. He or she makes many decisions. He or she talks to the president and to other members of the government. The Speaker needs to be a listener, too. This might be the most important thing! The Speaker listens to ordinary people talk about their lives and what they expect from Congress. Listening helps the Speaker make decisions. Talking and listening are both important.

"Ready for anything" describes the Speaker. In fact, he or she is in line for **succession**. This means he or she could become president. If the president dies, the vice president takes over as president. If the vice president also passes away, the Speaker is called. He or she must be very brave. Being the Speaker is a hard job. It is also an important job. Without the Speaker, the House might fall apart! No laws would be made. We need roles like the Speaker to keep the government running smoothly.

Serving the People

The Speaker serves many people. The Speaker works for his or her party. A party is a group of people with similar ideas. The Speaker also works for the members of the House. Most important, the Speaker works for ordinary people like you!

The Speaker of the House often answers questions from the press.

CHAPTER TWO

A Day in the Life of the Speaker of the House

The Speaker works on the House **floor**. This is where the members sit and where speeches are made. The Speaker helps make laws. He or she helps take votes. But the days are not boring. The Speaker has many different duties! He or she works on and off the floor. Each week, he or she runs all over Capitol Hill.

MORNING

John Boehner served as Speaker of the House. He did this from 2011 to 2015. At breakfast, he would read "everything there is to read." He read his schedule and **briefings**. Briefings are full of information. Around

Breakfast

John Boehner woke early for coffee. He went to his favorite diner, Pete's, for breakfast. Each day at Pete's, Boehner ate eggs and sausage. Then he felt ready to work. Many days, he opened the House. He told the members it was time to start.

9:00 a.m., he arrived at the Capitol. His team arrived at 7:30 a.m. They get there early! The team must prepare. They know the day will be long.

Each morning, Boehner read his memos. He also held a staff meeting. He gave his staff a "lay of the land." They talked about **bills**. Bills move through the House each day. Bills are ideas that could become laws.

AFTERNOON

The Speaker has no time to nap. Afternoons are all about meetings! He or she has daily meetings with the other

House leaders. The Speaker also holds meetings with other members of Congress, with his or her party, and with citizens. The Speaker reads letters and talks on the phone.

Some Speakers, such as Paul Ryan, have multiple offices for meetings. The Speaker skips most votes. Instead of voting, he or she has more meetings. A strong team must be in place. A whole team keeps the Speaker on schedule.

EVENING

A day in the Speaker's life is not short. After all those meetings, he or she may have to return to the House.

The President and the Speaker

The Speaker meets with members of Congress. He or she often meets with the president, too. Sometimes these meetings are last-minute. Other Speakers set up regular check-ins with the president. Some have even spoken daily!

President Obama and Speaker John Boehner met often.

There might be a late vote. The Speaker helps push his or her party's ideas through Congress. So the Speaker must talk to other members of Congress. He or she tries to get them to vote with his or her party. The Speaker might work to get a bill passed. He or she could also try to get laws **repealed**. This means they get canceled or reversed. The Speaker often needs to spend the evening preparing for the next day.

Taking Time to Relax

Paul Ryan is a strong Speaker—and a strong weight lifter!

The Speaker's days are long. At night, he or she finally gets to return home. To let off steam, Speaker Paul Ryan likes to work out. To relax, Speaker Nancy Pelosi enjoyed crossword puzzles. It is healthy to separate home time from work time.

Being the Speaker of the House is hard work, but it can also be fun.

CONCLUSION

The Speaker of the House doesn't have a steady routine. Business in Congress changes on a day-to-day basis. Some days are fast-paced. Other days are steady. The Speaker leads the majority party and runs the House. He or she attends meetings and events. The Speaker's week is packed. Each and every day is different!

Voters often display signs to show their support for certain candidates.

CHAPTER THREE

Becoming the Speaker of the House

Does the Speaker's job sound fun? One day, that could be you! Traditionally, you must first be a member of the House. All kinds of people work there. Usually, they start by working at the local level. Then they might work for the state government. The national level comes next.

We elect members to the **federal** House. These people's decisions affect the whole country. This election happens every two years. Some states have a few members in the House. Others elect many! It depends on the state's size. States with more people have more members.

You can run for the House when you are twenty-five. You must be a United States citizen. You also must live in the state where you run. Paul Ryan is from Wisconsin. He became Speaker in 2015. He lived in Wisconsin when he first ran for the House in 1998. He spoke to many people. He wrote letters. He raised money. And finally, he won!

In November, we have Election Day. Anyone who is eighteen or older can vote. First, you register. You fill out forms. Then, you fill out your **ballot**. This is the paper with all the candidates' names. Sometimes the ballot is on a

Special booths are set up to keep everyone's vote a secret.

screen. There are Republicans and Democrats. Sometimes there are people without a party. They are **independents**. There are also smaller groups, like the Green Party. But most winning candidates come from the two main parties. The winners get to be members of the House. This is a full-time job. Members move to Washington, DC. They work on Capitol Hill each day.

To be in Congress, you must work hard. You must meet many people. You have to introduce yourself. You need to share your ideas. To become the Speaker, you

The night of an election is full of emotions for the voters.

Congress has many members, all with different viewpoints.

work even harder! Everyone in the House helps choose the Speaker. They choose someone who will work hard. They elect someone who will listen and talk. They believe the Speaker will help them work well together.

In the House, there are two parties. Both parties choose options for Speaker. The party with the most members gets to elect the Speaker. This means they get to choose. Some years, the Republicans have more members. They choose. Other years, the Democrats have more. Then they choose. The Speaker changes with the party. After

Kids can hold elections, too!

he or she wins, the Speaker is sworn in. The dean swears the Speaker in. The dean has been in Congress the longest.

Usually, a person is Speaker until the next election. Sometimes he or she **resigns**, or quits. Then someone new becomes Speaker. The gavel is passed. This is a special moment. The Speaker of the House is a very special and important job.

The First Female Speaker of the House

More women are running for office and winning. The House has more women than ever! Nancy Pelosi was the first female Speaker. She started the job in 2007 and served for four years. She learned from her dad, the mayor of Baltimore.

People are always fighting for the Speaker's attention when he's at the Capitol.

CHAPTER FOUR

How Can You Get Involved?

Do you want to be the Speaker of the House? You can! Men and women can do the job. You could speak Spanish and English. You could be deaf. You could be short or tall. You could be anyone. *You* could be the Speaker!

The job is hard. You must talk and listen. You must meet with all kinds of people. You have busy days. You serve the Congress, your party, and citizens. It is hard to serve all three. But you could do it.

If you want to work on Capitol Hill, you can start now. Read the newspaper. Read articles online. Learn

City council meetings are great places to check out politics.

about your local government. On Election Day, your parents will vote. Go with them! You can watch them vote. You might even get a sticker. You can ask your parents about voting. Who did they vote for? Why did they pick that candidate? They might have strong feelings. Listen to their opinions. You can have your own opinions, too.

You can also go to town meetings. Many cities have town councils. These are like mini versions of Congress. You can go to the meetings. You can listen to plans for the town. You can even raise your hand to speak! Council members love to hear from residents. They love to hear from kids. Your opinion counts. You can make your voice heard!

Go to meetings. Write letters. Call your representatives. Their phone numbers are online. You can ask them questions. You can tell them what you think. What is important to you? Clean air? School? Roads? Equality? You can tell your representatives. It is their job to listen.

Does your school have an election? Get involved! Student government is fun. It is a great way to learn. You will listen to students. You will talk to teachers.

Does your school have a student government?

Someday, you could hold the gavel. You could lead the House of Representatives! The Speaker is a tough role, but it is important. The Speaker helps Congress function and move the country forward. We need a Speaker of the House. One day, it could be you.

Get Involved!

People who work in Congress want to help their communities. You can help, too! You can serve others at a shelter or soup kitchen. You can join Scouts or get involved at a church. Hold a bake sale for an important cause. Make signs and posters. Go to a march with your parents. Use your voice! It matters.

GLOSSARY

ballot A piece of paper or screen on which a person marks his or her vote.

bill A draft of a law presented to Congress for discussion.

briefing A detailed summary of important information.

committee A group of people with a specific function or goal.

federal Relating to the central government of the United States.

floor The place where members of Congress sit, have discussions, and vote.

gavel A small wooden mallet that is used to call for order.

independent An individual politician who is not connected to a party.

GLOSSARY

oath A promise about one's future actions or behavior.

party A group of people with similar ideas about government.

repeal To cancel or reverse a law.

resign To choose to leave a job or position.

succession The process of inheriting a job or title.

FIND OUT MORE!

BOOKS

Ragone, Nick. *The Everything American Government Book: From the Constitution to Present-Day Elections, All You Need to Understand Our Democratic System.* Avon, MA: F+W, 2004.

Spier, Peter. *We the People: The Constitution of the United States.* New York: Random House, 2014.

FIND OUT MORE!

Worth, Bonnie. *One Vote, Two Votes, I Vote, You Vote.* Cat in the Hat's Learning Library. New York: Random House, 2016.

WEBSITES

Ben's Guide to the United States Government
https://bensguide.gpo.gov

Kids.gov
https://kids.usa.gov

Kids in the House
http://kids.clerk.house.gov

MEET THE AUTHOR

Kaitlyn Duling believes in the power of words to change hearts, minds, and, ultimately, actions. A poet, nonfiction author, and grant writer who grew up in Illinois, she now resides in Pittsburgh, Pennsylvania, where she works aboard a bookmobile and helps kids learn to love to read. She knows that knowledge of the past is the key to our future and wants to make sure that all children and families have access to high-quality information. She loves to visit Washington, DC, and see the monuments. This is her fifth book for Cavendish Square.

INDEX